1853

MEET
Marie-G.

An American Girl

By SARAH MASTERS BUCKEY

ILLUSTRATIONS CHRISTINE KORNACKI

VIGNETTES CINDY SALANS ROSENHEIM

★ American Girl®

THE AMERICAN GIRLS

1764

KAYA, an adventurous Nez Perce girl whose deep love for horses and respect for nature nourish her spirit

1774

FELICITY, a spunky, spritely colonial girl, full of energy and independence

1824

JOSEFINA, a Hispanic girl whose heart and hopes are as big as the New Mexico sky

1853

CÉCILE AND MARIE-GRACE, two girls whose friendship helps them—and New Orleans—survive terrible times

1854

KIRSTEN, a pioneer girl of strength and spirit who settles on the frontier

1864      ADDY, a courageous girl determined to be free in the midst of the Civil War

1904      SAMANTHA, a bright Victorian beauty, an orphan raised by her wealthy grandmother

1914      REBECCA, a lively girl with dramatic flair growing up in New York City

1934      KIT, a clever, resourceful girl facing the Great Depression with spirit and determination

1944      MOLLY, who schemes and dreams on the home front during World War Two

1974      JULIE, a fun-loving girl from San Francisco who faces big changes—and creates a few of her own

Questions or comments? Call 1-800-845-0005, visit **americangirl.com**,
or write to Customer Service, American Girl, 8400 Fairway Place,
Middleton, WI 53562-0497.

Printed in China
11 12 13 14 15 16 LEO 10 9 8 7 6 5

Profound appreciation to Mary Niall Mitchell, Associate Professor of History, University
of New Orleans; Sally Kittredge Reeves, former Notarial Archivist, New Orleans; and
Thomas A. Klingler, Associate Professor, Department of French and Italian, Tulane University

This book is a work of fiction. Any similarity to real persons, living or dead, is coincidental
and not intended by American Girl. References to real events, people, or places are used
fictitiously. Other names, characters, places, and incidents are the products of imagination.

PICTURE CREDITS
The following individuals and organizations have generously given
permission to reprint images contained in "Looking Back":
p. 85—photo by Shelley Cornia; pp. 86–87—The Historic New Orleans Collection,
accession no. 1948.3 (Jackson Square); The Historic New Orleans Collection, accession
no. 00.37 (building exterior); The Historic New Orleans Collection, accession no. 1992.94 (dock);
pp. 88–89—The Historic New Orleans Collection, accession no. 1974.25.24.62 PC 24–2–A
(people in the park); Edmond Dédé, Louisiana Music Collection, Amistad Research Center at
Tulane University (free man of color); pp. 90–91—The Historic New Orleans Collection,
accession no. 1979.124 (ballroom); Picture Collection, The New York Public Library, Astor,
Lenox and Tilden Foundations (children in costume); p. 92—John Coletti/Photolibrary.

Cataloging-in-Publication data available from the Library of Congress

FOR JAY

In 1853, many people in New Orleans spoke French as well as English. You'll see some French words in this book. For help in pronouncing or understanding the foreign words, look in the glossary beginning on page 93.

Table of Contents

Marie-Grace's Family

PAPA
Marie-Grace's father, a dedicated doctor who is serious but kind

MRS. CURTIS
A no-nonsense widow who has been the Gardners' housekeeper for four years

MARIE-GRACE
A shy, caring nine-year-old girl who is happy to be back in New Orleans

UNCLE LUC
Marie-Grace's uncle, who is a Mississippi River steamboat pilot

ARGOS
Marie-Grace's dog, who is her constant companion

. . . AND FRIENDS

MADEMOISELLE
OCÉANE
*A French opera singer who
gives voice lessons*

LAVINIA
HALSWORTH
*A wealthy girl who
likes to be the boss*

CÉCILE REY
*A confident girl who
takes voice lessons with
Mademoiselle Océane*

HOME AGAIN

January 1853

Marie-Grace Gardner woke up to a strange sound coming through the window above her bed. She listened closely. Then she heard it again—the sweet, high notes of trumpets and the *rat-a-tat-tat* of drums.

She sat straight up in bed. *It's music,* she realized. *Maybe it's a parade!*

Marie-Grace loved parades, and Papa had told her that the parades in New Orleans were the best in the world. Marie-Grace could hardly wait to see if it was true.

She swung her feet onto the bare wood floor. Her big dog, Argos, had been curled up next to her bed. Now Argos lifted his head and looked at her through the gray fur that half covered his eyes. "Let's find Papa," she told him. Argos jumped up and hurried to the door.

The room wasn't see-your-breath frozen, as her room in Elton, Massachusetts, had always been in the winter. But it was chilly enough to raise goose bumps on her arms. Marie-Grace searched in her trunk for something to wear over her flannel nightgown. She and her father and their housekeeper, Mrs. Curtis, had arrived in New Orleans only the night before. So far, all she had unpacked were her blankets, her nightgown, and the small oval portrait of her mother that she always kept by her bed. She grabbed a wool shawl from the trunk and stepped out of her room.

"Papa?" she called. Her voice echoed through the hall. There was no reply.

Marie-Grace guessed that her father was unpacking his office. She and Argos climbed down the outside stairs to the open courtyard. The stones felt cold under her feet as she hurried to a door on the ground floor of the building.

"Papa," Marie-Grace began as she burst into her father's office, "I heard music outside and—"

She stopped suddenly. Her father, Dr. Thaddeus Gardner, was sitting at his desk. But he wasn't alone. A handsome man with a mustache was sitting across from him. *Papa must have a patient already,* Marie-Grace realized. "Excuse me, sir," she stammered and began to retreat toward the door.

But instead of following her, Argos yelped and rushed toward the man. For a moment, Marie-Grace was afraid he was going to jump up on the stranger. "No, Argos!" she cried.

The man just laughed. "Hello, my friend," he greeted Argos, and patted the dog's head. Argos wagged his tail so hard that it thumped against Papa's desk. The man stood up and grinned at Marie-Grace. "Ti-Marie," he exclaimed. "How wonderful to see you again! Why, you've grown to be the very image of your mama."

Marie-Grace stared at the stranger. Her mother's nickname for her had been Ti-Marie. But since Mama had died, no one had ever called her by that name. *Who is this man?* she wondered.

Her father stood up, too, and the sun from the

3

window behind him glinted off his wire-rim glasses. "Marie-Grace," he said, smiling, "you recall your Uncle Luc. He came to bring us a basket of food and welcome us home to New Orleans."

Marie-Grace nodded shyly. She had been born in New Orleans, but she had been away for so long that now she hardly recognized her uncle. He was her mother's youngest brother, and he worked as a pilot on a steamboat. When Marie-Grace and her parents and her baby brother, Daniel, had lived in New Orleans four years ago, Uncle Luc had often visited. Marie-Grace remembered him bringing news from Mama's family and treats from his trips up the river.

One summer, Uncle Luc had surprised Marie-Grace with a tiny gray puppy he had rescued and named Argos. Marie-Grace and Argos had been friends from their first day together. Whenever she had gone for walks with Mama and Daniel, or skipped rope in the courtyard, Argos had stayed close by her side. Marie-Grace remembered it as the happiest time of her life.

But that winter, a cholera epidemic had swept through the city. In one terrible week, Mama and Daniel had both died. Soon afterward, Papa had packed up his medical supplies and taken Marie-Grace and Argos away from New Orleans and back to Pennsylvania, where he had grown up.

Papa was a dedicated doctor, and he worked long hours taking care of the sick and the poor. But since many of Papa's patients couldn't pay, the Gardners were always short of money. During the last few years, they had moved from town to town in the Northeast, looking for just the right place for Papa to work. Moving had been hard for Marie-Grace. None of the places where they lived ever seemed as warm and welcoming as the home she remembered with Mama and Daniel in New Orleans.

Marie-Grace had been happy when Papa decided it was time for them to return to New Orleans. Yet now, everything was unfamiliar—even Uncle Luc. "How do you do, sir?" she mumbled, curtsying just as her mother had taught her so long ago.

"*Très bien*," exclaimed Uncle Luc. "Very well." He gave her a hug and a quick kiss on each cheek. Then he said something else in rapid-fire French. She stared at him blankly.

"We've been away so long that Marie-Grace has forgotten much of her French," her father told Uncle

Luc. "I'm afraid I'm a bit rusty, too."

Uncle Luc shrugged as if to say that whatever language they spoke was not important. "I told your papa that it's good you are back home in New Orleans. All our family is looking forward to seeing you again," he explained in perfect English. "I remember how much you enjoyed visiting everyone in Belle Chênière when you were little, and how brave you were!"

Marie-Grace was astonished. "Me, brave?"

"*Bien sûr,* of course," said Uncle Luc. "You begged your mama, my dear sister, to let you picnic by the bayou. She wisely said that there were too many alligators in the swamps for children to go exploring by themselves. But I will always remember my brave Ti-Marie—only four years old and you said, 'Alligators don't scare me!'"

Marie-Grace felt her face grow red while her father and Uncle Luc laughed together. She had a dim recollection of visiting Belle Chênière, the little town not far from New Orleans where her mother's family, the Rousseaus, lived. She remembered playing with her cousins and paddling in a boat. But she couldn't ever remember being brave.

Uncle Luc reached for his hat. "I must go and call upon a friend at the Royal Music Hall," he told them. "Why don't you both come with me? We could see the parades along the way."

Marie-Grace's eyes widened. "There really is a parade?" she asked, remembering the music she had heard.

"There are lots of them today," said Uncle Luc. "It's the anniversary of our victory at the Battle of New Orleans. The biggest parade will be on Canal Street—it's the best in the city."

Marie-Grace looked hopefully at her father. But he shook his head and gestured at the stacks of boxes that filled his office. "I'm sorry, Luc," he said. "I've too much to do here."

Marie-Grace stared down at the dusty floor. *I'll never get to see the parade*, she thought.

Her uncle seemed to read her mind. "Perhaps Marie-Grace could come to the parade with me?" he suggested to her father. "She ought to see the celebration, and I would like to introduce her to my friend who sings with the opera." Uncle Luc turned to Marie-Grace. "Do you still enjoy music, just as your mama did?"

"Oh, yes!" said Marie-Grace, her excitement overcoming her shyness.

To Marie-Grace's surprise and delight, Papa agreed to the plan. While Papa and Uncle Luc talked, she gulped her breakfast and quickly changed into her best wool dress and bonnet.

Outside in the bright January sunlight, Uncle Luc helped her into a hired carriage. "Please take us to Canal Street, Monsieur Bernard," Uncle Luc told the driver as they settled onto the leather seat. "This young lady would like to see the parade."

"*Certainement,*" said the driver, a broad-shouldered man with black hair and light brown skin. He flicked his reins and they were off, the clip-clop of the horse's hooves echoing against the stone paving.

Monsieur Bernard steered the carriage down narrow streets, past colorful homes with arched doorways and shuttered windows. Pretty iron balconies reached out from many of the houses, and Marie-Grace glimpsed walled courtyards behind the buildings. *Everything here is so different,* Marie-Grace thought as they drove past trees heavy with green leaves in the middle of winter.

Marie-Grace caught the scent of onions and herbs cooking, and she took a deep breath. The tempting, spicy smell wasn't at all like the plain foods Mrs. Curtis cooked. It reminded Marie-Grace of the stews her mother used to make long ago.

Soon the carriage turned onto a wide street that bordered the river. The street was bustling with people, and Uncle Luc said that the French Quarter, New Orleans' oldest neighborhood, was becoming busier every day. Buildings crowded one side of the street. On the other side was the majestic Mississippi River. Several steamboats churned up the river. Clouds of smoke and steam floated above the boats, and their high-pitched whistles pierced the air.

Dozens of sailing ships and riverboats were docked along the levee. Uncle Luc pointed out his steamboat, the *Eléanore*, which was piled high with crates of cargo. "It's one of the fastest boats on the river," he said proudly.

"And look over there—there's Jackson Square," said Uncle Luc as they passed a large square filled with gardens. "It's General Jackson's victory in 1815

that we're celebrating today. The people in New Orleans fought back the British to protect the city."

On the other side of the square, Marie-Grace saw a towering white building with three spires

that reached to the sky. It reminded her of a picture in a fairy-tale book. "Is that a castle?" she guessed.

"No, that's St. Louis Cathedral," Uncle Luc said, smiling. "Beautiful, isn't it? And soon you'll see the parade!"

When they reached Canal Street, Marie-Grace and her uncle stepped out of the carriage and joined the crowds lining both sides of the street. Some of the spectators were wedged in doorways, and others stood along the edge of the road waving handkerchiefs and American flags.

Marie-Grace stared in amazement. The parade was far grander than anything she had ever seen before. Row after row of soldiers marched by in carefully pressed uniforms, their swords swinging by their sides. A group of white-haired men who had fought in the Battle of New Orleans marched proudly, too. As the men passed by, the crowd

10

cheered wildly, drums beat out the rhythm, and horns blared from the brass bands. The music was so thrilling that Marie-Grace wished she could march along, too. *New Orleans must be the best city in the world*, she thought, her toes tapping to the music. *Surely it has the best parades! I wish Papa was here to see this, too.*

After the last drummers passed by, pounding a thunderous beat, Uncle Luc gave Marie-Grace his arm. Together they made their way up Canal Street along a raised sidewalk, which Uncle Luc called the *banquette*. He was telling Marie-Grace an exciting story about pirates who once lived in New Orleans when a man called, "Mr. Rousseau! A word with you, please!"

Uncle Luc stopped and tipped his hat. Then he introduced Marie-Grace to Mr. Halsworth, a plump, well-dressed man, and his daughter, Lavinia, who looked slightly older than Marie-Grace.

As Mr. Halsworth talked with Uncle Luc about shipping cotton on the *Eléanore*, Marie-Grace smiled hesitantly at the other girl. "It was a wonderful parade," Marie-Grace ventured.

Lavinia did not smile back. She surveyed Marie-

Grace's plain dress and bonnet with a critical eye. "I can't be bothered with parades," she replied.

Marie-Grace's face grew hot with embarrassment. *Did I say something wrong?* she wondered.

Lavinia wrapped herself in her fur-lined cloak. "I prefer *private* parties and balls where only the *best* in society are invited," she added. Then she thrust out her chin and turned to her father. "May we go now, Father?" Lavinia pleaded. "My friend Sophronia is expecting me."

Mr. Halsworth checked the heavy gold pocket watch that hung from his waistcoat. "Very well," he said. Then he and Lavinia walked briskly away without even saying good-bye.

Uncle Luc shook his head as he watched them leave. "It seems as if they are in quite a rush—and on a holiday, too."

"I don't think Lavinia liked me," Marie-Grace confessed. "She says she prefers the 'best in society,' but I'm not sure what that is."

"Don't worry about Lavinia," Uncle Luc advised as he and Marie-Grace continued along the banquette. "The Halsworths may judge others by how much money they have. But plenty of people will be friendly to you, if you are friendly to them. I'm sure you'll find lots of friends in New Orleans."

Marie-Grace was silent. During the last few years she had moved so many times that it had been hard for her to make any friends at all. *Maybe it will be different here,* she told herself.

"We'll take a shortcut to the music hall," said Uncle Luc as they turned a corner. Compared to the bustling crowds on Canal Street, this narrow street was quiet—almost deserted.

Suddenly, Marie-Grace heard a man's harsh voice yell, "Stop, you!" She whirled around. Behind her, two burly white men grabbed a black boy of about fourteen or fifteen.

"Let me go!" the boy protested loudly. Then he said something in French that Marie-Grace did not understand.

The larger of the two white men shook the boy by the collar. "You look like the slave who ran away from Gray's Plantation," the man shouted at him. "Show us your papers."

Marie-Grace's heart beat fast. She turned back to her uncle, whose face was suddenly serious. "We go this way," he told Marie-Grace. He steered her away from the men and into an alleyway where the buildings were so close together that they nearly blocked out the sun.

When they were out of earshot, Marie-Grace asked, "Why did those men stop that boy? Did he do something wrong?"

"They think he's an escaped slave," Uncle Luc explained. "But the boy said he and his whole family are *gens de couleur libres*."

Marie-Grace looked up at him, puzzled. "Free people of color," her uncle translated. "In New Orleans, not all people of color are slaves. Many are free, and they have some of the rights that white people have."

In the years she had spent in the Northeast, Marie-Grace had not known many people of color, free or slave. But she'd often heard her father say that slavery was wrong, and he believed that all people should be treated equally.

"If that boy is free, why did those men stop him?" Marie-Grace asked.

Uncle Luc shrugged. "They wanted to check his papers. People of color have to carry papers to prove they are free."

Marie-Grace frowned. "I don't understand."

"Some free people of color are wealthy," Uncle Luc explained. "They own businesses and big houses, and they have their own society. But many others are not rich and if they're suspected of being escaped slaves, they have to show papers to show they're free. So, for that boy's sake, I hope he has papers."

I hope so, too, thought Marie-Grace, remembering the fear in the boy's eyes.

At the end of the alleyway, Uncle Luc led Marie-Grace to the back of an imposing stuccoed building. "*Bonjour,* Louis," Uncle Luc greeted the man at the door. "Is Mademoiselle Michel in?"

"*Oui,* Monsieur Rousseau, she's with a student," said the elderly watchman, waving them inside.

"Mademoiselle Océane Michel is French, and she trained in Paris," said Uncle Luc as they climbed the stairs. "She has the most beautiful voice! Besides singing in the opera in New Orleans, she gives lessons to talented young students."

I'm going to meet a real opera singer! Marie-Grace thought. Her hands were damp with nervousness as she held on to the banister.

When they reached the upstairs hall, Uncle Luc

stopped in front of a tall door. Marie-Grace heard a shrieking noise that sounded like someone trying to sing a high note—and failing miserably. *Is that what Uncle Luc means by talented students?* she wondered.

Uncle Luc glanced over at Marie-Grace, and then he covered his ears. Marie-Grace started to giggle, and Uncle Luc burst into a deep, hearty laugh.

Suddenly, the singing stopped. The door swung open. A girl about Marie-Grace's age glared at them.

Marie-Grace stopped laughing. *What have I done now?* she wondered.

JUST THE RIGHT NOTE

The elegantly dressed girl stood in front of Marie-Grace, blocking the entrance to the music studio. The girl was holding a sheaf of music, and her eyes were blazing.

"Why are you laughing?" the girl demanded.

Uncle Luc composed his face immediately. "Bonjour, mademoiselle," he said seriously. "I laughed because my niece looked so astonished when she heard the music coming from within this room." Uncle Luc gestured toward Marie-Grace. "She seemed quite impressed!"

The girl gave Uncle Luc a doubtful look. With a swish of her pink dress, she turned to Marie-Grace.

"Really?" the girl asked.

Marie-Grace did not want to lie. She thought for a moment, wondering how she could be both honest and kind. "I've never heard anything like it," she said finally.

A slender young woman joined them at the door. Her face lit up when she saw Uncle Luc, and he took her hand for a moment. Then with a bow, Uncle Luc said, "Mademoiselle Océane, I would like to introduce my niece, Marie-Grace Rousseau Gardner."

"Your uncle has told me much about you, Marie-Grace," said Mademoiselle Océane with a friendly smile. She had fair skin and chestnut brown hair held back with a silver comb. Her blue-green eyes were the color of the ocean. "I am so pleased to meet you at last." She reached out her hand to Marie-Grace.

Marie-Grace felt a happy blush fill her face as she shook hands with Mademoiselle Océane. She had never imagined that a real opera singer would be so welcoming.

Mademoiselle Océane gestured toward the girl who had opened the door. "Monsieur Rousseau,

18

Marie-Grace, I'd like you to meet one of my favorite students, Cécile Rey."

Uncle Luc bowed politely to the girl and then turned to talk with Mademoiselle Océane. Marie-Grace stood awkwardly for a moment. Cécile had warm brown skin, and Marie-Grace guessed that she was a free person of color. *What should I say to her?* Marie-Grace wondered. Then she remembered how Papa always said that all people should be treated the same. So Marie-Grace followed Mademoiselle Océane's example. "I'm pleased to meet you," she said as she held out her hand to the other girl.

For a moment, Cécile just looked at her. *Oh no!* thought Marie-Grace. *I've done something wrong again!*

Then Cécile reached out and took Marie-Grace's hand. "Hello," Cécile said with a smile.

Marie-Grace smiled back. Cécile had sparkling hazel eyes, and her dark hair was styled in long, loose curls. Her lace-trimmed dress reminded Marie-Grace of Lavinia's fancy clothes. *She seems nicer than Lavinia*, Marie-Grace thought with relief.

As Uncle Luc and Mademoiselle Océane chatted together in French, Marie-Grace tried to think of something more to say to Cécile. She wanted to

"Hello," Cécile said, smiling warmly. Marie-Grace smiled back.

be friendly, just as Uncle Luc had suggested, but it was so hard to overcome her shyness. "It must be wonderful to learn how to sing here," she said finally.

Cécile's smile grew brighter. "Oh, it is," she replied in French-accented English. "Mademoiselle Océane is the best teacher. She is very patient and understanding—even when I make mistakes! My *maman* wants me to learn to sing well, and Mademoiselle makes me believe that I will someday." Cécile smiled again. "Does your maman want you to take lessons, too?"

"No," said Marie-Grace, looking away. It was still hard for her to talk about Mama. "My mother passed away when we first lived in New Orleans—when I was little."

Cécile reached out and touched Marie-Grace's arm. "I am very sorry," she said softly, and Marie-Grace felt warmed by her kindness.

"My uncle passed away a short time ago," Cécile said. "I know my cousin misses him very much. René—that's my cousin—and my Aunt Octavia came back to live with us in New Orleans." Then Cécile brightened. "So you were born here, too? But you sound like an American."

Marie-Grace was confused. "I *was* born in New

21

Orleans," she said. "But I *am* American. Aren't you?"

"I'm from New Orleans!" Cécile answered proudly, as if that explained everything.

Marie-Grace frowned. Wasn't New Orleans part of America? What about the American flags she had seen waving at the parade? "Isn't that the same thing?" she asked Cécile.

"No," said Cécile, shaking her head. "New Orleans is different from anywhere else in America. And people from New Orleans are different from people anywhere else, too! My grandfather says so, and he has been all around the world."

Marie-Grace thought about her trip through the city with Uncle Luc. "It *is* exciting," she agreed. "Compared to all the other places I've lived, New Orleans *does* seem like a different world."

"You've traveled?" Cécile asked. "Where have you been? I can't wait to travel and have adventures."

"Oh, we moved a lot, but I never had *adventures*," Marie-Grace admitted.

"Tell me about all the places you've lived," Cécile encouraged her.

Marie-Grace's shyness began to melt away as she described the quiet town of Elton, which boasted a small inn, a general store, and three shops. Cécile listened closely and asked lots of questions. Then she told Marie-Grace about her own home in the French Quarter, where she had lived all her life.

"You already have adventures," Marie-Grace said after Cécile described her pet parrot flying around a parlor full of people. "And you're lucky that you haven't had to move. Moving is hard."

Cécile started to say something when a pink-cheeked girl opened the door and stepped in. The girl bobbed a curtsy and, speaking with a lilting Irish accent, she apologized to Mademoiselle Océane for the interruption. Then she turned to Cécile.

"Miss Cécile," she said, "we'd best get your things. Be quick. The carriage is waiting."

"Yes, Ellen," Cécile answered. She looked at Marie-Grace. "Our maid is here to take me home. Perhaps we'll see each other again," Cécile said with a grin. "I hope we do." Then she threw on her cloak while the maid gathered her gloves and several sheets of music.

"*Au revoir*, Marie-Grace!" Cécile called over

her shoulder as she and Ellen hurried out together. "Good-bye."

"Au revoir," Marie-Grace replied, and she suddenly realized she was speaking French.

Mademoiselle Océane turned to Marie-Grace. "Your uncle tells me that you love music," she said, her eyes twinkling. "He thinks perhaps you might enjoy singing lessons."

Marie-Grace felt her heart thumping inside her chest. "I *do* like to sing," she admitted. "But I don't know how—not really."

"Let's see," said Mademoiselle Océane. She sat down on the piano stool and handed Marie-Grace a sheet of paper. "Sing these scales, please."

Marie-Grace looked at the lined paper. It had been a long time since she'd had music lessons, and she couldn't make sense of the marks that looked like strangely shaped *o*'s and *p*'s and *d*'s. She shook her head. "I'm not very good at reading music."

"Follow after me," said Mademoiselle Océane. She played a single note on the piano. Then, in a clear, beautiful voice, she sang, "La, la, la, la, la, la, la, la!" Each note rose higher than the last, like steps on a staircase.

Blending her voice with Mademoiselle Océane's, Marie-Grace sang the scale several times. Then she and Mademoiselle Océane tried singing a short song together. At first Marie-Grace was embarrassed. But the more she sang, the more she lost herself in the music.

When the song ended, Uncle Luc applauded. Then he turned to Mademoiselle Océane. "What do you think?"

Marie-Grace held her breath, waiting for the answer. "She needs training," Mademoiselle Océane said slowly. "And she'll have to learn to read music properly. But she has a good ear and a lovely voice. I would be happy to teach her—if, of course, her father permits."

Marie-Grace breathed a happy sigh. *I have a lovely voice,* she repeated to herself. *And if Papa agrees, I can take lessons with Mademoiselle Océane.* The sun shining into the room seemed brighter than ever.

When Marie-Grace arrived home, Argos ran to greet her, his tail thumping. She hugged him and whispered, "Let's go find Papa. I have good news."

But when she and Argos entered her father's office, it was empty. All Marie-Grace found was a note from her father saying that he had gone out to buy supplies and would be back before supper.

Marie-Grace hurried up the outside stairs to the family's living quarters. Mrs. Curtis, a stout woman with iron-gray hair, was scrubbing the floor with a liquid that smelled like vinegar. Papa had hired Mrs. Curtis to keep house for them when they lived in Pennsylvania, and she had traveled with them ever since. Mrs. Curtis always grumbled whenever she had to set up housekeeping in a new place. She wouldn't rest until everything was sparkling clean.

Mrs. Curtis greeted Marie-Grace with a sniff of disapproval. "I'm glad you're finally back, missy," she said. "You can help me get things in order. Goodness knows we have enough to do."

Marie-Grace's excitement faded. Whenever Mrs. Curtis was in a good mood, she called her "dearie." But whenever Mrs. Curtis had chores for her, Marie-Grace was "missy." With a sigh, Marie-Grace took off her cloak and changed into her work dress and apron. For the rest of the afternoon, she and Mrs. Curtis swept, scrubbed, and sorted. By the time Papa returned, the dining room was clean, the dishes were unpacked, and there was a fire crackling in the fireplace.

"Why, this looks like a feast!" Papa proclaimed as he and Marie-Grace sat down to an evening meal of soup, bread, and cheese, all supplied by Uncle Luc.

"I suppose this is all right to eat," Mrs. Curtis said doubtfully as she ladled out the soup. "Mr. Rousseau told me it's called 'jumbo,' or something like that. He seemed to think you'd like it."

"It's shrimp gumbo," said Dr. Gardner with a smile as he handed Marie-Grace a bowl. "And it used to be one of your favorite foods, Marie-Grace."

Marie-Grace breathed in the rich aroma. It reminded her again of her mother's cooking. She took a sip of the steaming broth. "It's delicious!"

"If you ask me, it's got too many spices," muttered Mrs. Curtis.

"People here in New Orleans like lots of flavor in their food," said Dr. Gardner, with a wink to Marie-Grace. He took another sip of his soup.

Marie-Grace paused as she savored the gumbo. Then she remembered how Cécile had wanted to know if she was from New Orleans or if she was

"American." "Papa, New Orleans *is* part of America, isn't it?" she asked.

"Yes, of course," said her father. "The French founded New Orleans, then Spain controlled it, and then it belonged to France again. But it's been part of America for nearly fifty years now, ever since the Louisiana Purchase."

"Then why do so many people here talk like foreigners?" asked Mrs. Curtis as she sliced the bread. "It seems like half the folks hardly talk English!"

Dr. Gardner helped himself to the crisp bread. "Many families have lived in Louisiana for generations," he explained to Mrs. Curtis, "so they speak French just as their parents and grandparents did." He turned to Marie-Grace. "Your mama was very proud of her French heritage. Her parents were quite surprised when she told them that she wanted to marry an American from Pennsylvania. The Rousseaus considered *me* the foreigner. But in time, they came to accept me. And I'm very glad they did."

"That reminds me," said Mrs. Curtis, frowning. "Mr. Rousseau brought something called pecan pie. I'll go get it."

While her father buttered his bread, Marie-Grace

told him all about the parade and her visit to the Royal Music Hall. "I met a girl named Cécile today. She's taking singing lessons with Mademoiselle Océane. May I take lessons, too, Papa? Mademoiselle Océane says she'll teach me if you say yes."

Papa paused, his knife still in the air. "Your mother always said you had a good ear for music. I suppose I've neglected your lessons, haven't I?" He put down the knife. "I'll ask Mademoiselle Océane what her fees are. Then we'll see what might be possible."

"That would be wonderful!" exclaimed Marie-Grace. She reached for his hand across the table. "I'll practice every day."

Papa patted her hand, and then he pushed back his wire-rim glasses. "I think it's also time for you to attend a regular school," he continued. "Your uncle reminded me that St. Teresa's Academy is just a few blocks from here. It's one of the best girls' schools in the city. Your mother thought very highly of it."

Marie-Grace was speechless. Because they had moved so much, she had never gone to any school for more than a few months. When she hadn't been in school, Papa had made sure she kept up with her lessons by teaching her at home in the evenings. If

Papa planned to enroll her at St. Teresa's Academy, it meant that he also planned to stay in New Orleans. *I could go to school every day,* Marie-Grace realized. *I could even make friends with girls my age.* The possibility seemed almost too good to be true.

Mrs. Curtis came back into the dining room with the pie. "A girl can learn all she needs to know at home," she declared. "Too much schooling fills a girl's head with useless nonsense."

"Thank you, Mrs. Curtis," Dr. Gardner said firmly. "But Marie-Grace is an intelligent girl, and I think St. Teresa's will be just the place for her." He turned to Marie-Grace. "As soon as we're settled, I'll see about enrolling you."

Marie-Grace sang to herself as she went to bed that night. The room was chilly, but as she tucked herself under the blankets, she felt a warm sense of

contentment. She looked at the miniature portrait of her mother. "I'm glad we came back to New Orleans, Mama," she whispered. "I just hope we can stay."

CHAPTER
THREE
—

A HELPING HAND

On Monday morning, Marie-
Grace helped her father hang
his medical license in his office.
Then they carried an old chair outside to the front
of the building. Standing on the chair, Papa hung
his wooden sign on an iron hook above the office
window. The sign announced in faded silver letters:

Dr. Thaddeus Gardner
Physician

"Does that look right?" he called to Marie-Grace.
"It's perfect," she said.
"Well, then," said Papa, stepping down and

surveying his new office, "we're truly open for business."

There was still plenty of work to do to get the office ready. Papa used live worms called leeches in some of his medical treatments, and the leeches needed fresh water every few days. Marie-Grace didn't like looking at the squiggly worms, so she cleaned their jars as quickly as she could. She was carefully putting a jar on a shelf when the bell over the front door clanged loudly.

"Our first patients!" Mrs. Curtis announced. Smiling, she hurried to the front room. But when the housekeeper returned, her smile had vanished. "It's just a couple of ragged little boys," she reported. "They don't speak English, and I'll bet they don't have a penny to their names. I don't think they're the kind of patients you want, Dr. Gardner."

The lines in Papa's forehead deepened. "Anyone who needs help is welcome here, Mrs. Curtis. Please show the boys in."

Mrs. Curtis scowled. But she came back a moment later with two dark-skinned boys. The older boy, who looked about eight years old, pushed a skinny younger boy into the room. The child stumbled in without a word. He was holding tightly to a cloth wrapped around his arm, and tears were streaming down his face.

In rapid French, the older boy pleaded for help. The only words Marie-Grace understood were *mon frère*, "my brother," and *arbre*, "tree." She wondered if the younger boy had fallen from a tree.

Papa lifted the boy up to the examining table. Then he unwrapped the cloth around the child's arm. Blood flowed onto the office floor, and the boy began to sob. "Marie-Grace, get me the sutures," her father said crisply.

"I'd better get the mop," said Mrs. Curtis, shaking her head.

Marie-Grace ran for the curved needles and catgut thread that her father used to sew up wounds. She tried to thread a needle with a long, sinewy strand of catgut. But as the boy's sobs grew louder, her hands started to shake and she kept missing the eye of the needle.

Her father glanced up from cleaning the boy's wound. "Steady, Marie-Grace," he advised her. "You can do it, if you stay calm."

Marie-Grace took a deep breath. Then she tried

one more time. This time, the catgut went through the tiny opening. She handed the needle to her father.

With quick, neat stitches, her father sewed up the gash on the boy's arm. Then he covered another smaller cut with sticking plaster. The boy's sobs finally quieted. He looked more curious than scared as he stared down at the plaster on his arm. Marie-Grace felt almost weak with relief.

"I don't suppose we have any sweets in the jar, do we, Marie-Grace?" her father asked, looking around at the office's half-empty shelves.

Marie-Grace shook her head. "Not yet, Papa."

"No matter," said her father. He reached into his pocket and gave the boys a penny. Then, in careful French, he told them how to care for the injured arm.

"*Merci*. Thank you," the older boy said. Then he hurried his little brother out of the room.

Mrs. Curtis finished wiping the floor. "I thought you were supposed to *get* money from patients—not *give* it to them," she muttered as she carried the mop out of the room.

After Papa finished putting away the sticking plaster, he turned to Marie-Grace. "Thanks to your

*The boy looked more curious than scared as he stared down at
the plaster on his arm.*

help, we got that boy stitched up before he lost too much blood," he said. "I'd say the practice is off to a good start, wouldn't you?"

Marie-Grace was cutting another length of catgut. She wanted to have a needle ready the next time her father needed her help. Her hands were steady now, and she easily slipped the catgut through the needle's eye. Smiling, she looked up at her father. "Yes indeed, Papa."

Over the next few days, Marie-Grace assisted her father in his office and helped Mrs. Curtis with chores. Every morning, Marie-Grace and Argos went with Mrs. Curtis to the French Market, a busy open-air market just a few blocks from their home. Mrs. Curtis walked slowly because her knees were stiff with arthritis. Sometimes the housekeeper would get so tired that she'd stop to rest on a bench outside the market. Then Marie-Grace would offer to do the shopping for her.

Marie-Grace loved exploring the market. Near the entrance, Choctaw Indian women wearing beautiful beaded necklaces sold *filé* powder for gumbos. There were women with bright kerchiefs around their heads selling dried peppers and spices. Some of the women were dark-skinned and some were light-skinned, and they called out to customers in French mixed with English and  Spanish. Beyond the entrance were rows and rows of vegetables such as sweet potatoes and beets, and fragrant fruits including mandarins and lemons. There were pastries and fresh-baked loaves of bread called *baguettes*, along with savory cheeses, jams and jellies, jars of pickles, and many other foods.

Marie-Grace wished she could stroll slowly through the market and see everything. But Mrs. Curtis did not like the crowds of "foreigners," as she called them, and as soon as she had their groceries, she was in a hurry to go home. One sunny morning, however, Mrs. Curtis discovered that they had left the market without buying bread and potatoes.

"I'll go back for them," Marie-Grace offered eagerly.

Mrs. Curtis frowned. "Alone?"

"I used to go to the shops in Elton by myself,"

Marie-Grace reminded her. "And I won't be alone. Argos will be with me."

Mrs. Curtis thought for a moment. "I guess you can go just this once," she said finally. "But remember, New Orleans is a whole lot bigger than Elton. Watch out when you cross the streets. And don't talk to strangers!"

Marie-Grace promised that she'd be careful, and she and Argos hurried back to the market. When they crossed the streets, Marie-Grace stayed well away from the horses trotting by. She felt proud of herself when she arrived at the bakery stall. She smiled at the baker, a red-faced man with a big mustache, and said in her best French, *"Une banquette, s'il vous plaît."*

The baker's mustache twitched with a smile. Then Marie-Grace heard someone giggling behind her. She turned around and was surprised to see Cécile, the girl from Mademoiselle Océane's studio. Cécile said something to an older woman at her side. The woman nodded and moved on to a stall of vegetables, and Cécile darted over to Marie-Grace.

"Marie-Grace," said Cécile, still giggling. "You really should work on your French. It's *baguette*, not *banquette!*"

Suddenly, Marie-Grace realized that she'd asked the baker for a sidewalk instead of a loaf of bread. For a moment she was so embarrassed that she wished she could sink into the ground. Then she saw that Cécile was smiling as if they had shared a good joke.

Marie-Grace laughed. "I'm not very good at French," she admitted. She paid for the baguette and tucked it into her basket. "Maybe I'll learn more when I start school."

"You're going to school?" Cécile asked with interest.

"Yes," said Marie-Grace, brightening. "My papa says I may be able to take lessons with Mademoiselle Océane, too."

"Oh, I hope so," Cécile said eagerly. "Perhaps we will see each other there." She glanced at Marie-Grace's basket, and then she looked around the market. "Are you here with your cook?"

Marie-Grace shook her head. "No, I'm here with Argos."

"Is Argos your maid?" asked Cécile.

Argos had been sniffing under a table, but when he heard his name he trotted over. His tail was wagging, and he thrust his head toward Cécile as if he was sure she'd want to pet him. *"This* is Argos," Marie-Grace explained proudly.

"He's enormous!" cried Cécile. She jumped back as Argos peered into her market basket. "Will he bite?"

"No! He likes you," said Marie-Grace, and she smiled as Argos nuzzled Cécile's hand.

Cécile laughed. "No, he smells my *pralines.*"

"What are pralines?"

"They're my favorite sweet. Haven't you ever tried one?"

Marie-Grace shook her head. "I don't think so."

"Here, have two," said Cécile, and she gave Marie-Grace two brown sweets dotted with pecans.

"Mmm," said Marie-Grace as soon as she took a bite. "Of course, pralines! My mother used to buy these for me when I was little. How could I have forgotten? Thank you." Marie-Grace carefully wrapped the second praline in her handkerchief so that she could share it with Papa when she got home.

"Are you really here with just Argos?" Cécile asked. "I'm not ever allowed to go farther than our courtyard by myself."

"Oh," said Marie-Grace, surprised. She glanced around the crowded market and realized that all the wealthy girls like Cécile had servants with them. The only girls her age who were shopping alone looked as if they were housemaids.

"I run errands for our housekeeper, Mrs. Curtis. And for my papa, too, sometimes," Marie-Grace told Cécile. She explained that in Elton, she had often shopped by herself at the pharmacy and the general store. "But if I don't get home soon, Mrs. Curtis will worry. Come with me to the next row so that I can get potatoes."

"I can't," Cécile said. "Our cook, Mathilde, will be looking for me. But remember, this is the French Market. Ask for *pommes de terre*, not potatoes."

Marie-Grace nodded. She was about to say "thank you" but caught herself. "Merci," she said as she waved good-bye.

From then on, whenever she went to the market, Marie-Grace watched for Cécile, but she never saw her. So Marie-Grace spent the next few days helping Mrs. Curtis and playing with Argos in the courtyard. She had hoped that Papa might have more time to spend with her once he was settled into his new office. But Papa began working long hours, and Marie-Grace often had to wait up in the evenings if she wanted to see him.

She was lonely when Papa was gone, and she looked forward to the afternoons when he let her go with him to visit patients. A few times they traveled by hired carriage to a neighborhood where large houses were set far back from the streets. Elegant gardens surrounded these houses, and tall trees bent over the wide avenues, like graceful dancers taking their bows.

More often, though, her father went to neighborhoods where immigrants from Ireland, Germany, and other countries lived in cramped tenements. He would not allow Marie-Grace to go with him on these visits.

"It's too dangerous," Papa told her. "In such crowded conditions, diseases can spread like fire in a cotton warehouse."

"What about you, Papa?" asked Marie-Grace. "I don't want you to get sick."

"I'm always careful," he promised. "And I wouldn't be much of a doctor if I never went to see my patients, would I?"

Papa was so busy that Marie-Grace didn't want to bother him. But she worried that he had forgotten all about her music lessons. Then, one evening at supper, he mentioned that he had talked with Mademoiselle Océane.

"You may begin your lessons on Saturday," her father announced between bites of ham and sweet potatoes.

"Thank you, Papa!" Marie-Grace exclaimed joyfully. She had a sudden vision of herself singing with Mademoiselle Océane in the sun-filled room. *Maybe I'll see Cécile,* she thought. *We might even be able to sing a song together and—*

Her father's voice broke into her thoughts. "I have more good news," he continued. "This morning, I hired a maid to help Mrs. Curtis with the housework, and I enrolled you at St. Teresa's Academy."

Marie-Grace put down her fork. She'd been excited about the idea of school. But now that she was actually enrolled, she felt a nervous flutter in her stomach. "When will I start?"

"First thing tomorrow," Papa said with a smile.

IMPORTANT
LESSONS

The next morning, Marie-Grace was so nervous that she could barely swallow the porridge Mrs. Curtis had made. Before she left home, Marie-Grace gave Argos a long hug. "I'll miss you when I'm at school," she whispered to him. "But I'll be back this afternoon, and I'll tell you all about it."

It was raining, so Papa held an umbrella over her as they walked together to St. Teresa's. "I think you'll like this school, Marie-Grace," he said. "And I'm sure you'll make friends here, too."

Marie-Grace hoped with all her heart that her father was right. She thought of how nice Cécile had been at the French Market. But she also remembered her encounter with Lavinia Halsworth. *What will the girls at St. Teresa's be like?* Marie-Grace wondered.

Her father walked her through the school's iron gate and up to the wide front door. A freckled young nun welcomed them to the school. Marie-Grace's mouth felt dry as she said good-bye to her father. She followed the nun down a wood-paneled hall that smelled of chalk dust.

The nun stopped at the last door. "You'll be here, in Sister Pauline's class," she announced. Marie-Grace stepped into the classroom as quietly as she could.

A tall nun with spectacles was standing at the front of the room, lecturing to the class. Three rows of girls sat facing the teacher. All of the students turned around when the door closed behind Marie-Grace. As the girls stared at her, Marie-Grace felt the blood rush to her face. She suddenly realized two awful facts.

First, Sister Pauline was lecturing in French.

Even worse, Lavinia Halsworth was sitting in the front row.

The first few moments passed in a blur. Sister Pauline rapped on her desk. Then she looked straight at Marie-Grace and asked her a question in French.

The room was silent. Marie-Grace sensed that everyone was waiting for her to reply, but her mind was blank. It was bad enough not to know the answer to a teacher's question. She didn't even know what the question was. All she could think of to say was the French word for "yes."

"Oui?" she said hopefully.

As soon as the word was out of her mouth, Marie-Grace heard ripples of laughter. She knew that she had given the wrong answer, and she wished she could run out the door, back to Papa.

Sister Pauline rapped again on her desk, and the laughter stopped. Then she asked in English, "What is your name, please?"

Marie-Grace felt her blush deepen as she realized that was the question Sister Pauline had asked her the first time. She mumbled her name, and Sister Pauline smiled at her kindly.

"Take a seat, Marie-Grace," the nun directed. "And follow along as best you can."

As the other girls turned to face the front of the room, Marie-Grace looked for a place to sit. The only empty seat was in the middle row, at a double desk next to a skinny girl with curly brown hair.

Marie-Grace quickly slid in next to the girl.

"We're on this page," murmured the girl, tilting her book so that Marie-Grace could see it. When Marie-Grace glanced down at the page, she felt her stomach flip-flop. It was all written in French.

Lavinia whispered something to a girl with red hair. When the girl burst into giggles, Sister Pauline frowned at her. "Silence, please, Sophronia. You may welcome our new student at lunchtime. Now, let's return to our French lesson."

As the class continued, Marie-Grace struggled to follow along. She found herself recognizing some French words and phrases, but not nearly enough to understand the lesson. She was relieved when Sister Pauline taught the arithmetic lesson in English. *At least I can understand this,* Marie-Grace thought as she read the problems Sister Pauline wrote on the board. Papa had taught her arithmetic at home, and whenever she went shopping, she had to add and subtract in her head. Now Marie-Grace discovered that while other girls in the class seemed to be struggling, she solved the problems easily.

The hardest test came at lunchtime. The rain had stopped, and Marie-Grace took the basket that

Mrs. Curtis had packed and followed the other girls
out to the courtyard. It was a pleasant space, with
a view of the gardens and the stables in back of the
convent. There were benches arranged around a

 fountain, and the girls gathered in
tight clusters, talking and laughing.

On one bench, girls from
the back of the classroom were
chattering together in French.
Marie-Grace did not want to
embarrass herself by trying to speak French again,
so she continued past them.

Lavinia, Sophronia, and three other girls from
the front row were sitting together and chatting in
English. Marie-Grace smiled hopefully at them as
she approached the group. But when Lavinia saw
Marie-Grace, she spread out her skirt so that there
was no extra room on the bench. Marie-Grace
continued walking.

On the farthest bench, she found the girl with
curly brown hair whose books she had shared in
class. The girl was studying her spelling lesson and
eating a biscuit by herself. Marie-Grace stopped in
front of her.

The girl glanced up. "You can sit here if you want," she said with an Irish accent. "But you might not want to."

"Why not?" Marie-Grace asked.

With a bounce of her curls, the girl jerked her head toward Lavinia and her friends. "All the rich American girls who live in fancy houses sit over there." Then she gestured toward the other bench. "And all the girls from New Orleans sit over there. They talk French so fast that nobody else can understand them."

Marie-Grace thought for a moment. She wasn't sure that she fit in with either group. Even though she'd been born in New Orleans, she couldn't speak French very well. But she wasn't a rich American who lived in a fancy house, either. "I guess I'll sit here," she told the curly-haired girl and settled next to her.

Marie-Grace learned that the girl's name was Frances and that she had been at St. Teresa's for only two months. Frances's father was a builder, and he and his men were repairing the convent's stables.

"My pa's going to be finished here in a couple of weeks," said Frances. "Then our family's leaving New Orleans, and I'll never have to see those rich, snobby girls again." She frowned at Lavinia and her friends. "I can hardly wait till we move."

I never want to move again, Marie-Grace thought. She glanced over to the other bench where Lavinia chatted happily with her friends. *I'll have to try to get them to like me,* she decided. *Otherwise I'll be alone here.*

During the next week, Marie-Grace began to settle into the school routine. She liked Sister Pauline, and, except for French, she did well in her class work. Her favorite subject was arithmetic. When Sister Pauline called on her to solve problems at the blackboard, she almost always got the right answers. But one problem Marie-Grace couldn't solve was how to make friends with Lavinia Halsworth.

Lavinia boasted about being the best student in the class. She was often the first to raise her hand when Sister Pauline asked a question. On Tuesday, during their geography lesson, Sister Pauline asked what the capital of Pennsylvania was. Lavinia's hand shot up. "Philadelphia!" she answered.

Sister Pauline shook her head, and then she called

on Marie-Grace. For a moment, Marie-Grace hesitated. She knew the answer, but didn't want to seem as if she was showing off. Finally she mumbled, "Harrisburg?"

"Very good," said Sister Pauline, smiling.

"Lucky guess!" Lavinia whispered angrily. Marie-Grace tried to sink out of view.

At lunchtime, Marie-Grace sat with Frances, who usually read a book while she ate. Lavinia always sat in the middle of her front-row friends like a queen surrounded by her admirers. Marie-Grace listened to Lavinia talk loudly about her new dresses, the operas she attended, and most of all, the parties she was invited to.

"I have the most wonderful costume for Mardi Gras," Lavinia announced to her friends. "You'll never guess what I am going to be."

"You *have* to tell us," exclaimed Sophronia. "I already told you that I'm going to be an angel."

"You were an angel last year," Lavinia pointed out. "That's nothing special. But nobody's ever had a costume like mine before."

The girls begged Lavinia for hints about her costume, but she refused to give any details. "It's a secret," she teased.

Marie-Grace wished she could join the conversation. *What is Mardi Gras?* she wondered. *And why do they need costumes?*

But whenever Marie-Grace tried to talk to the front-row girls, either at lunchtime or in the classroom, Lavinia made it clear that she wasn't welcome.

One Friday afternoon, however, Marie-Grace thought her chance had come. Sister Pauline wrote several problems on the blackboard for the girls to solve, and then she stepped out of the room.

Sophronia studied the problems. "I don't understand this one at all," she announced, and she read aloud from the board. "If Mary has one dollar, and she goes to the market and buys two pounds of flour for five cents a pound, how much money will Mary have left?"

"How should *I* know how much money Mary has?" Sophronia wailed, staring at her blank slate. She turned around to Marie-Grace. "Do *you* know how to solve it?"

"I think so," said Marie-Grace, happy that Sophronia wanted her opinion. "You begin by figuring out the total cost of the flour—"

Lavinia turned and glared at Marie-Grace.

"That's not right," she interrupted.

Marie-Grace shrank back in her seat. "It isn't?"

"No," Lavinia said triumphantly. "You *begin* by sending your maid to do the marketing." Lavinia laughed loudly at her own joke, and the other girls in the front row laughed, too. Even Sophronia giggled.

Lavinia gave her friend a scornful look. "Honestly, Sophie, it's an easy problem," she said, snatching Sophronia's slate away from her. "*I'll* show you how to do it."

As Marie-Grace bent over her own work, she heard Lavinia whisper to her friends, "Some girls think they know *everything*, but they can't even speak French. All they can say is, 'oui, oui, oui!'"

The other girls giggled again, and Marie-Grace felt her face burn. *How will I ever make friends here?* she wondered with a sinking heart.

Every week at school, Marie-Grace looked forward to Saturdays. At exactly ten o'clock in the morning, she and Argos set off for the Royal Music Hall. They walked side by side under the pretty iron

*At exactly ten o'clock in the morning, Marie-Grace and Argos
set off for the Royal Music Hall.*

balconies that reached out over the banquettes. When they neared Jackson Square, the smell of roasting coffee beans and steamed milk was everywhere. The cafés were full of customers, and the markets were crowded with shoppers. As they walked, Argos kept close to Marie-Grace. No matter how busy the streets were, he stayed by her side. He didn't even chase the pigeons when they crossed Jackson Square.

"Good dog," Marie-Grace said as birds fluttered around them. "Good dog!"

Louis, the watchman at the music hall, had become friends with Argos. Louis often saved treats for the big dog, and Argos sat with him by the back entrance while Marie-Grace went upstairs to Mademoiselle Océane's studio.

Today, Cécile's lesson ended just as Marie-Grace arrived. Marie-Grace waited outside the studio until Cécile finished. Cécile rushed out with a big smile and said, "Bonjour, *comment vas-tu?*" Then she repeated herself in English. "Hello, how are you?"

Marie-Grace smiled and answered in English, "I'm very well, thank you. How are you?" Then she practiced her French with Cécile, who gently corrected her pronunciation and taught her new words and expressions. *I wish the girls at school were as kind as Cécile,* Marie-Grace thought.

All week, Marie-Grace looked forward to seeing Cécile. The two girls never ran out of things to talk about. Cécile told Marie-Grace about her busy household, her lessons with her tutor, and her pet parrot. Marie-Grace, in turn, told Cécile about helping her father in his office, Mrs. Curtis's grumblings about cooking "strange New Orleans foods," and Argos's latest adventures.

"I'm sorry we cannot talk longer," Cécile always said when Ellen came to fetch her. Marie-Grace was sorry, too. It was time for her own lesson next, though, and it was wonderful to sing with Mademoiselle Océane.

The lesson was fun, but it was also hard work. Marie-Grace had to stand up straight, breathe properly, and sing scales—lots and lots of scales. When Mademoiselle introduced a new song, she and Marie-Grace would sing it together, going over and over the hard parts. The hour went quickly, and Marie-Grace was always surprised when the clock struck eleven-thirty. "*Bon!* Good! Enough for today," Mademoiselle Océane would say. "Now, Marie-Grace, would you like some tea?"

"Yes, please," Marie-Grace would reply. She loved talking with Mademoiselle Océane, and they had become friends outside the studio, too. When Uncle Luc's steamboat had been in New Orleans recently, he had brought Mademoiselle Océane to the Gardners' house for tea. Since Papa and Marie-Grace hardly ever had guests, it had been a special occasion. Marie-Grace had been allowed to wear her best dress and serve little iced cakes to everyone.

Today Mademoiselle smiled as she poured a cup of steaming hot tea for Marie-Grace. "I am so happy," she said. "Your uncle wrote that he will be back in New Orleans in time for the Mardi Gras balls!"

Marie-Grace put a lump of sugar into her tea. "I've heard girls at school talking about Mardi Gras. What is it?"

"Mardi Gras means 'fat Tuesday,'" Mademoiselle explained. "We have dances, parties, and wonderful food on Mardi Gras, because it's the last day before the holy season of Lent begins. Then after the forty days of Lent, of course, we celebrate Easter."

"Oh," said Marie-Grace, still a bit confused. She remembered how Lavinia had boasted about her secret costume. "Does everyone dress in costumes?"

Mademoiselle nodded. "Many people spend weeks planning what they will wear," she said. "The balls are very grand events. There are even special balls for children."

"Really?" exclaimed Marie-Grace. She had read about fancy balls in fairy tales. She imagined how exciting it would be to go to one—especially a costume ball. "It sounds wonderful."

"Yes," Mademoiselle agreed. Then she set her teacup down carefully in its saucer. "But you need an invitation to attend. Perhaps, though . . ." Mademoiselle's voice trailed off.

Marie-Grace did not wait for her to continue. She knew that invitations were for girls like Lavinia, who lived in fancy houses and belonged to the "best society." Marie-Grace shrugged. "I would never know what to do at a ball, anyway. And I'd never have a costume to wear, either."

"Do not say 'never,'" Mademoiselle chided her gently. "Mardi Gras is magical—you never know what might happen." Her blue-green eyes sparkled as she pulled a piece of paper from her music book. "Now, here is your uncle's letter, *chérie*," she said.

"He sends his love to you and says he will take us both for a carriage ride when he returns. He is a very nice man, *non?*"

"No—I mean, yes!" Marie-Grace agreed. She had a sudden happy thought. "Are you and Uncle Luc going to get married?"

Mademoiselle's cheeks went bright red. "It is too soon to talk of such things," she protested. But she was smiling as she put Uncle Luc's letter away.

By Special Invitation

The following Saturday, Marie-Grace was bursting with news.

She was so excited that she bolted down her breakfast and raced through her chores. Then she and Argos hurried to the music hall.

They arrived well before the usual time. While Argos stayed with Louis, Marie-Grace bounded up the stairs to the second floor. Through the closed door of Mademoiselle's studio, she could hear Cécile practicing the same line of music over and over. As soon as she was sure that Cécile's lesson was done, Marie-Grace opened the door.

"Mademoiselle! Cécile!" she greeted them. "The most wonderful thing has happened."

Marie-Grace pulled a heavy square of parchment paper out of her cloak and showed it to them. "Last night, a messenger brought this. It's an invitation to the Children's Opera Ball, and it's addressed to me!"

"I am so glad it arrived," said Mademoiselle, her face wreathed in smiles.

Marie-Grace stared at her in surprise. "You knew about it?"

Mademoiselle nodded, her eyes twinkling. "Yes. My friend Gabrielle was helping with the list of invitations, and I asked her to send you one. The Opera Ball is one of the best children's balls of the season, so you should have a wonderful time. I think I have a costume that will be perfect for you, too."

For a moment, Marie-Grace was speechless. She was thrilled to be invited to the costume ball, and now she knew that Mademoiselle Océane had arranged the invitation just for her. Marie-Grace felt a lump in her throat. Papa loved her and he was kind, but this was the first time since Mama had died that anyone had made her feel so cherished.

"Thank you," she said finally, holding the invitation close to her heart. "Thank you so much."

"You are welcome, chérie," Mademoiselle replied.

"I thought you might like a special treat."

Marie-Grace felt a happy glow until she looked at Cécile. Her friend was frowning fiercely and sorting her sheet music so roughly that the music stand shook.

"Cécile?" Mademoiselle Océane asked. "Whatever is the matter?"

Cécile settled the sheet music on the stand with a thump. "What about me, Mademoiselle? Don't I get a special treat, too?" she burst out. "I've been your student longer!"

Marie-Grace did not understand. Cécile was always so confident and bubbling with happiness. She had a loving family, a maid to watch over her, lots of friends, and even a parrot that talked. *Surely she can't be envious of me,* Marie-Grace thought.

"Cécile, calm yourself," said Mademoiselle Océane. Then she added gently, "You and I have shared many special times, too. And you go to a lovely Mardi Gras ball every year, non?"

"Oui," Cécile admitted. She studied the floor for a moment before she looked up at her teacher. "I'm sorry, Mademoiselle."

Cécile turned to Marie-Grace. "I was very rude

just now," she said, blinking back tears. "Please forgive me."

"Yes, of course," said Marie-Grace instantly.

"Your news *is* wonderful," Cécile continued. "Mardi Gras is truly magical. You'll see."

Marie-Grace's excitement began to return. She glanced at the fancy invitation in her hands. "So, are you coming to the Children's Opera Ball, too, Cécile?" she asked hopefully.

"Why, no," Cécile said, sounding surprised. Then, seeing the puzzlement on her friend's face, she explained, "I *am* going to a ball. But we free people of color have our own separate Mardi Gras parties and balls."

Marie-Grace looked from Cécile to Mademoiselle and back again. "Why?" she asked. Here in New Orleans, white people and people of color lived on the same streets and shopped at the same markets. Couldn't they go to the same Mardi Gras balls?

"Because . . ." Cécile shrugged. "It's always been that way."

Marie-Grace frowned. It would be such fun if she and Cécile could enjoy Mardi Gras together. "I wish we could go to the same ball," she said, half to herself.

"Girls!" called Mademoiselle Océane, lightly tapping her baton on the piano to get their attention. "This year both balls will be held at the same place on the same evening." She smiled. "Perhaps you will see each other. Now, Cécile, shall we help Marie-Grace choose her costume?"

Mademoiselle gestured toward the far end of the room, where a pair of trunks sat half-hidden by a Chinese screen painted with dragons. "Why don't you look in that first trunk?" she suggested. "It has the fairy costumes that children wore in *The Magic Flute.* I'm sure one will fit you, Marie-Grace. You may try them on behind the screen."

Marie-Grace searched through the cedar-scented costume trunk until she found several sparkling gowns with masks and delicate matching fairy wings. Cécile helped Marie-Grace gather up an armful to try on.

Marie-Grace took the fairy costumes behind the screen. She soon discovered, however, that trying on costumes was harder than she had expected. There were laces to be tied and confusing buttons to be buttoned. She was glad Cécile was there to help. Finally, Marie-Grace found a costume that fit just right. She stepped out from behind the screen.

Marie-Grace searched through the trunk until she found several sparkling gowns with masks and delicate matching fairy wings.

Cécile clapped her hands. "It's *magnifique.*"

"It *is* magnificent—you look beautiful, Marie-Grace!" agreed Mademoiselle. "I wish your papa were here to see you."

Marie-Grace hurried over to the tall mirror that stood in the corner. When she saw her reflection, she breathed a sigh of happiness. The silver shone in the light, and when she spun around, the delicate fairy wings fluttered on her back. As Marie-Grace looked into the mirror, she remembered the fairy tales her mother used to read to her. For a moment, she could almost imagine her mother standing behind her smiling.

"Thank you, Mademoiselle. And you, too, Cécile," she said, turning to face them. "I never dreamed of such a beautiful costume."

"But you must get dressed now, Marie-Grace," Mademoiselle reminded her. "It's past time for us to start your lesson."

"Go on," Cécile said. "I'll put the costumes away." She gestured to the shimmering wings and gowns.

Marie-Grace thanked her and quickly changed back into her own clothes. She was already working on her second song by the time Cécile finally came out from behind the Chinese screen. Cécile waved a cheerful good-bye as she hurried out the door.

I can hardly wait for Mardi Gras, Marie-Grace thought as she hit her highest note.

On the evening of the Children's Opera Ball, Marie-Grace waited by the window in her father's office. Papa had promised to be home by six o'clock so that he could take her to the ball. Now it was past six-thirty, and there was still no sign of him. Marie-Grace peered out the window, looking in every direction. Then she paced up and down the length of the office, her crisp petticoats crackling.

"Do you see him yet?" Marie-Grace asked Mrs. Curtis.

"Not yet," said Mrs. Curtis with a sigh. "And that's the fifth time you've asked me. Now settle down, dearie. You look very nice, and your father will be home soon, I'm sure."

Marie-Grace continued to pace as the minute hand of the big clock inched forward. At ten minutes to seven, she asked Mrs. Curtis if she could walk to the ball by herself. "Argos can come with me," Marie-Grace pleaded. "We walk to the music hall every Saturday."

"No," Mrs. Curtis said firmly. "It's not proper for a girl your age to be out by herself at night. If my arthritis weren't so bad, I would walk you over there myself, but as it is—"

Suddenly, the doorknob rattled, and Marie-Grace breathed a sigh of relief. But when the door opened, it wasn't Papa. It was only a boy. He handed Mrs. Curtis a folded note. "Message for you, ma'am."

Mrs. Curtis, who had never learned to read, passed the note to Marie-Grace. Marie-Grace read aloud the short scrawled message from her father: "Can't leave patient."

But Papa promised, Marie-Grace thought in despair. She turned away so that Mrs. Curtis would not see the tears welling in her eyes.

Then she heard Mrs. Curtis's firm voice. "Bring us a cab, boy," she ordered the messenger. "And be quick about it."

Marie-Grace spun around, amazed.

"Well, I can't have you miss the ball altogether, can I now?" the housekeeper said gruffly. "I may be

68

old, but I still remember how exciting it is for a girl to go to her first dance."

Mrs. Curtis took off her apron and put on her bonnet and cloak. Marie-Grace quickly gathered up her invitation and her mask. A few moments later, a carriage pulled up in front of the office.

As they bounced along the stone-paved streets, Marie-Grace could hear fireworks and music echoing through the French Quarter. *Oh, I hope I'm not too late,* Marie-Grace thought anxiously.

"Go along and enjoy yourself, dearie," said Mrs. Curtis when the carriage lurched to a stop in front of the Grand Théâtre. "I'm sure your father will be back in time to fetch you. And if he's not, I'll come myself."

"Thank you," said Marie-Grace as she jumped out of the carriage. "Thank you very much."

The early evening was getting dark, and men were lighting the streetlamps. Marie-Grace held tightly to her invitation as she rushed up the wide marble steps of the theater. Her first ball was about to begin!

CHAPTER
SIX

SWITCHED

Inside the theater, chandeliers shed sparkling light everywhere. The lobby smelled of perfume, and it was full of partygoers in fancy costumes. Marie-Grace looked around, unsure where to go next. From a landing, two staircases branched upward to the floor above. A pair of boys dressed as soldiers hurried up the right-hand staircase, their toy swords clanking. *They must be going to the costume ball, too,* she thought, and she followed them.

On the second floor, a pair of glass doors led to a balcony. The doors were partly covered by curtains. Through a gap in the fabric, Marie-Grace could see fireworks light up the sky like falling stars.

70

But the boys did not stop to admire the view. They turned right. Marie-Grace followed them down a wide hall where three sets of double doors, each attended by a pair of uniformed footmen, opened into a single spacious ballroom. Marie-Grace could hear an orchestra playing a spirited polka, and excitement bubbled up inside her.

A woman in a gold gown asked to see her invitation. Marie-Grace gave her the engraved parchment, and the woman smiled and gestured her toward the double doors.

Marie-Grace put on her mask and stepped into the ballroom. Crystal chandeliers gave a soft glow to the elegant room, and she saw children in all kinds of fancy gowns and suits. Marie-Grace could tell what some of the costumes were—there were shepherdesses, soldiers, princesses, and jesters. But some of the costumes were unlike anything she had seen before. Around the edges of the room, children gathered in clusters, talking and laughing. In the center of the polished floor, dozens of dancers were swirling in circles in time to the music.

As costumed children skipped and twirled by, Marie-Grace recognized Sophronia and Lavinia.

Sophronia's angel costume was topped with a halo that shimmered on her red hair. Lavinia was wearing a shiny green gown with a narrow skirt and a long train in the back. *That must be her secret costume,* realized Marie-Grace. *I wonder what it's supposed to be.*

Lavinia wasn't wearing a mask, and Marie-Grace saw her make a face at another girl, who swung the wrong direction in the polka. Marie-Grace decided that she would join the next dance at the other end of the ballroom, as far from Lavinia as she could possibly get. She edged her way through the crowd, past tables filled with platters of delicious-looking sweets. Marie-Grace had never seen so many treats. She took off her mask and nibbled a delicately frosted petit four.

Two blond girls were standing in the corner, half-hidden by a huge crystal punch bowl. Marie-Grace smiled at them hesitantly. The girls smiled back. They were both wearing simple blue dresses with white aprons and caps.

"What a beautiful fairy costume!" said the taller girl, looking admiringly at Marie-Grace's wings.

"Thank you," said Marie-Grace. Then she

paused. She wasn't sure what the girls were dressed as, and she was afraid to make the wrong guess.

The girl noticed her confusion. "My sister and I are dairymaids," she explained.

"We're just visiting New Orleans," the younger girl added. "We've never been to a ball before." She looked around. "Are all the balls here this . . . this fancy?"

Marie-Grace's toes were tapping as she watched the dancers weave back and forth. "I don't know," she answered. "This is my first ball, too. I can't wait to dance."

The polka ended, and there was a pause in the music. As the dancers helped themselves to refreshments, Lavinia passed by. She was wearing a green crown that matched her shiny green dress. When she saw Marie-Grace, she stopped short. "Why are *you* here?" Lavinia demanded.

Marie-Grace felt her face turn red. "I was invited," she said shyly.

"Indeed?" said Lavinia. Her eyes swept over Marie-Grace's costume. "You don't look too bad," she admitted. "But lots of girls are fairies. I'm the only mermaid queen!"

Lavinia twirled around, and Marie-Grace realized that the long green train was supposed to be a mermaid's tail. "It's very pretty," Marie-Grace said politely. "Is it hard to dance in?"

"Not at all," Lavinia replied with a shrug that suggested she had been dancing in mermaid tails all her life. "Of course," she continued, "I've been to *lots* of balls and I know *all* the dances. If you've never been to a ball before, I warn you not to dance tonight."

Marie-Grace swallowed hard. "Why not?"

Lavinia waved a green-gloved hand at Marie-Grace. "You are a *newcomer*," she said with a sigh. "And the dancing is really only for families who are part of society and who know just what to do."

Marie-Grace saw the blond girls exchange a nervous glance. "I didn't know that," said Marie-Grace, blushing even harder. She was confused. "I have an invitation, so I thought—"

"Of course you can *watch* the dancing," Lavinia interrupted. "And if you'd like some sweets or punch, I suppose that would be all right," she added with a half smile. Then, with a swish of her mermaid tail, she walked off to join the other dancers.

74

Marie-Grace watched Lavinia, Sophronia, and other girls line up opposite the boys. Marie-Grace wanted to line up, too. *But what would Lavinia do if she saw me dancing?* Marie-Grace wondered. *She would probably make fun of me in front of everyone—just the way she does at school.*

The fiddlers began to play a cheerful tune, and Marie-Grace could not stand still any longer. She walked around the edge of the dance floor to the other side of the room, where she stood in the doorway watching. The music went faster and faster, and the costumed dancers laughed as they struggled to keep up. Some of them missed steps, but they all looked as if they were having a wonderful time. Marie-Grace ached to join them.

Suddenly she felt a tap on her shoulder. She turned around. Another fairy—her mirror image—was standing behind her. With a wave of her gloved hand, the fairy beckoned to Marie-Grace.

Marie-Grace's heart was pounding as she followed the other fairy out of the ballroom. The woman in the gold dress was gone, and no one noticed the two fairies hurrying down the hall together. When they reached the staircase, the other fairy pushed aside the curtains, opened the doors, and motioned to Marie-Grace. Both girls stepped out

 onto a tiny balcony that overlooked a courtyard.

Marie-Grace felt as if she were looking at her twin. "Cécile?" she asked. "Is that you?"

"Surprise!" Cécile exclaimed. She pushed her mask back from her face and Marie-Grace could see that Cécile was delighted with herself.

Suddenly, Marie-Grace realized why Cécile had taken so long behind the Chinese screen at Mademoiselle's studio. She had borrowed a fairy costume as well.

"No one could tell us apart!" Marie-Grace said breathlessly.

"I know," said Cécile, her face bright with excitement. "I have a plan. *I* want to see what the Children's Opera Ball is like, and *you'll* get to go to two Mardi Gras balls."

In a low voice, Cécile quickly explained her idea: Marie-Grace would go to Cécile's ball at the other end of the hall, and Cécile would go to Marie-Grace's ball. After one dance, they would meet back at the balcony and then return to their own balls. "It will be easy," Cécile concluded.

Marie-Grace took off her mask and turned it nervously in her hands. "I wasn't invited to your ball," she reminded Cécile.

"*I* am inviting you," said Cécile confidently.

"I don't know," said Marie-Grace. She felt her heart thumping. "You said that the balls for white people and people of color are always separate. Won't we get into trouble if we switch places?"

"You were the one who wished we could go to the same ball," Cécile reminded her. "I want to find out what makes the Opera Ball so special. And we won't get into trouble because no one will ever know. It will be our secret."

Marie-Grace bit her lip. She had never met a girl as daring as Cécile. And now Cécile seemed to think that Marie-Grace was bold enough to join her! But what if the swap was more dangerous than Cécile admitted? *What should I do?* Marie-Grace wondered as she stared out over the courtyard.

"Come on," Cécile said. "It will be an adventure. It will be *our* adventure."

Just then, a burst of fireworks exploded in the
sky, and the colors floated in the air like fairy dust.
Marie-Grace remembered how Cécile had said that
Mardi Gras was magical. *If I'm ever going to be brave,*
she told herself, *this is the time.* She turned to Cécile.
"I'm ready."

Each girl put on her mask. Then, after checking
to be sure that the hall was still empty, they slipped
back into the building. "Remember," Marie-Grace
whispered, "just one dance." Cécile nodded and
waved her gloved fingers at Marie-Grace.

Marie-Grace followed Cécile's instructions and
found the other ballroom on the opposite side of the
theater. As she approached, she heard music. She saw
a pair of elderly ladies sitting together on a bench
outside the door.

What if they stop me? she wondered, and her
hands felt damp inside her gloves. But the ladies were
busy chatting with each other, and they didn't even
look up as she passed.

Inside, the candlelit ballroom was filled with
music, laughter, and conversation. The orchestra
sounded just as grand as the one at the Children's
Opera Ball, and the room looked just as elegant.

Bowls of punch and platters of delicious sweets were arranged on the linen-covered tables, and the polished floor was crowded with dancers wearing costumes. In the flickering candlelight, it was hard to tell if their skin was dark or light or some shade in between.

When the music ended, the boys bowed and the girls curtsied. Yet before the dancers could catch their breath, the violins started up again. Marie-Grace tapped her foot as she watched new lines of dancers form on the floor.

A tall girl dressed in endless yellow ruffles appeared at her elbow. "Come on, the music is starting," she said.

Before Marie-Grace could reply, the girl pulled her onto the dance floor. The tempo of the music picked up, and Marie-Grace found herself swept into a turning circle of dancers. She tried to follow the steps, but even when she made mistakes, no one seemed to notice. Everyone was having too much fun. As Marie-Grace whirled around, the silver wings on her costume fluttered. *This is wonderful*, she thought.

All too soon the music ended. Marie-Grace

longed to stay, but she remembered her agreement with Cécile—just one dance. "Pardon me," she murmured as she hurried through the crowded ballroom toward the door. "Excuse me."

She ran down the hall to the balcony at the top of the stairs and then slipped behind the curtains. She took her mask off, and a moment later, Cécile arrived.

"You were right," Marie-Grace told Cécile with a grin. "It *was* an adventure. I had a better time at your ball than I did at mine. And I danced!"

"I danced, too," said Cécile, lifting her mask.

The grin faded from Marie-Grace's face. "Oh, no," she whispered, remembering Lavinia's strict instructions. *I should have warned Cécile not to dance.*

But Cécile was smiling proudly. "Yes, even though a bossy girl told me not to."

Marie-Grace felt dread in the pit of her stomach. "What was the girl wearing?"

"Pooh," said Cécile with a shrug. "She was dressed in green. She looked like an alligator."

"What did you do?" Marie-Grace asked anxiously.

"I just laughed and kept on dancing. You should

have seen the look on her face," Cécile giggled.

All the confidence Marie-Grace had felt at Cécile's ball faded. "We'd better go back," she whispered to Cécile.

"Oui," Cécile agreed. "We can talk more at our lessons. Now we have our Mardi Gras secret to share." She reached out and gave Marie-Grace a quick hug. *"Bonne nuit.* Good night."

Marie-Grace's heart was warmed by Cécile's hug. "Bonne nuit," she replied, and she watched her fairy twin run down the hall. *She's not scared of anyone or anything*, Marie-Grace thought as Cécile disappeared from view. Marie-Grace put her mask back on and then headed down the hall to face Lavinia.

As soon as she entered the ballroom, Marie-Grace spotted Lavinia on the other side of the dance floor. The green crown and shiny green dress stood out among the crowd of costumes. When Lavinia caught sight of Marie-Grace, she narrowed her eyes and glared at her as if to say, *You're in trouble.*

Marie-Grace looked at her and saw that Cécile was right. Lavinia—with her angry eyes, her jutting chin, and her shiny green dress—really did look like an alligator. *She's not a mermaid queen at all,*

Marie-Grace realized. *She's not any kind of queen. She just thinks she is.*

The idea of Lavinia dressed up as an alligator was so silly that Marie-Grace started to giggle. Then she laughed out loud. Suddenly, she wasn't afraid at all. She felt as light as the fairy wings she was wearing.

A tall man in a black suit called out, "Ladies and gentlemen, please line up for the last dance of the evening, the Virginia reel!"

Marie-Grace hurried to the corner where the sisters in matching blue dresses still stood by the punch bowl. "Let's join in," Marie-Grace urged them. "We don't have to listen to that other girl. We can dance if we want to."

The sisters looked at each other and then turned to Marie-Grace. "Are you sure?" the older one asked.

"Yes," said Marie-Grace. "*I'm* inviting you."

Marie-Grace headed for the center of the ballroom floor. After some hesitation, the sisters followed her. A boy dressed as a pirate stood across from Marie-Grace. He bowed to her as the fiddles played the opening bars of the Virginia reel. Marie-Grace curtsied to the pirate boy. Then, smiling broadly, she stepped out in time to the music and began to skip and whirl across the ballroom floor.

When the ball was over, Marie-Grace found her father waiting in the lobby. Unlike the other grown-ups, who were arriving at the hotel dressed in costumes for their own dances, Papa was still wearing his work clothes, and he was carrying his medical bag.

"Hello, Grace," he greeted her. "Your fairy dress looks lovely. I'm sorry I couldn't get home in time to bring you to the ball. A little boy at Holy Trinity Orphanage was sick, and I needed to help him."

"Don't worry, Papa," Marie-Grace reassured him. "Mrs. Curtis and I managed just fine."

Just then, Cécile passed them on the steps. She was walking between two elegantly dressed grown-ups, and Marie-Grace guessed they were her parents. Cécile turned and waved to Marie-Grace before she stepped into a waiting carriage. Marie-Grace waved back happily. She could hardly wait to see Cécile at their next lesson—they had so much to talk about.

"Did you have a good time at the ball?" her
father asked as they strolled along in the cool, damp
evening air.

"Oh yes," said Marie-Grace, tucking her arm
into her father's. "There was beautiful music, and
I danced!"

"And who is that girl—the one you waved to, the
one whose costume looks just like yours?" he asked.

"Her name's Cécile," said Marie-Grace, smiling.
"And she's my friend."

LOOKING BACK

NEW ORLEANS
IN
1853

Marie-Grace lived in the French Quarter, the oldest part of New Orleans. This image from 1855 shows Jackson Square, the heart of the French Quarter.

When Marie-Grace arrived in New Orleans in 1853, she felt as if she'd stepped into a different world. People spoke French. Music with African and Caribbean rhythms spilled from the public squares. Spanish-style buildings opened to shaded courtyards filled with lush tropical plants. The city bustled with excitement, as though a parade or party was about to begin.

New Orleans *was* different from the rest of America. To begin with, the city had never belonged to England. It was founded by the French and was ruled by France or Spain for almost 100 years. The United States bought New Orleans as part of the Louisiana Purchase in 1803.

Many French Quarter buildings had European details, such as decorative iron balconies and wide arched doorways.

At that time, the city's residents were a more *diverse*, or mixed, group than those in the rest of America. Native Americans and people from France, Spain, Africa, and Canada had lived together from the very start of New Orleans' history. Each group's culture and customs mixed with the others to create a unique way of life.

New Orleans was also unique because of its location. Its position near the southern end of the Mississippi River made it an important port. Steamboats, like the one Marie-Grace's Uncle Luc piloted, brought cotton, sugar, and other crops down the Mississippi River and into New Orleans. The crops were then loaded onto ships and sent to the eastern United States, Europe, and the Caribbean. From across the ocean, luxuries such as spices, fabrics, and fine jewelry arrived in New Orleans. Boats like Uncle Luc's delivered that cargo up the river, where it was sold throughout the United States.

The docks in New Orleans were always busy. Workers unloaded cargo, and travelers got their first glimpse of America's largest Southern city.

By the 1830s, New Orleans was second only to New York City as the most important center for trade in America. With so much business in the city, more and more people from other parts of the United States moved to New Orleans. Immigrants from Ireland, Germany, and other parts of Europe arrived as well.

Newcomers—especially the Americans—were surprised at some New Orleans customs. Most people from the North, for example, believed Sunday was supposed to be a day of rest. After going to church, they did not travel or attend social events. People from New Orleans, on the other hand, enjoyed a European tradition called *Continental Sunday*. They went to church in the morning. Then they shopped at outdoor markets, attended parties, went to the theater, and even gambled. These were perfectly acceptable Sunday pastimes in New Orleans. But in the rest of America, they were considered shocking. One visitor from New England commented that people from New Orleans "keep Sunday as we in Boston keep the Fourth of July."

A Sunday stroll through the park was the perfect way to see friends and admire fashions from France.

Free people of color contributed to the culture of New Orleans as artists, writers, and musicians. Edmond Dédé was a famous violinist and composer.

Another thing newcomers found surprising was the large community of free people of color in New Orleans. In 1853, nearly a quarter of the city's population was of African heritage. Some were slaves, but thousands were free people of color, or *gens de couleur libres* in French. Like Cécile's family, many free people of color were well educated and well-to-do. They owned property and ran their own businesses. In New Orleans more than in other large cities in America, people of different races and colors lived in the same neighborhoods. They shopped in the same stores and attended the same religious and cultural events—though they sat in separate sections of churches and theaters. Free people of color were not treated equally with whites in New Orleans, but they had more freedom and opportunity than black people anywhere else in America.

Part of the reason for this freedom was that the governments of France and Spain had allowed slaves to earn money and buy their freedom. Free people of color also came to New Orleans from the French colony of Saint-Domingue (now the nation of Haiti). As these groups mixed and had families, they maintained ties to their African heritage as well as their European heritage. They were proud of their unique identity and built strong communities.

The social scene in New Orleans was as vibrant and varied as the people who lived there. The city was full of elegant theaters, so residents and visitors enjoyed operas, plays, ballets, and concerts. People browsed in fancy shops and dined in fine restaurants. They took carriage rides through the city and strolled along the levee. Sporting events and horse races were popular. People in New Orleans were fond of parties, and they adored music. Most of all, they loved to dance. A visitor from France commented that "in the winter they dance to keep warm, and in the summer they dance to keep cool." Balls were held throughout the week, and Sunday was an especially popular day for dancing. The grandest balls occurred during *Carnival* (kar-nee-vahl).

The French brought the custom of celebrating Carnival to New Orleans in the early 1700s. Carnival began on *Twelfth Night*, twelve days after Christmas, and ended on *Mardi Gras*, the Tuesday before Ash Wednesday. In French, Mardi Gras means "fat Tuesday." It is a day of feasting, merriment, and lots of dancing.

Some children's balls started at three o'clock in the afternoon and went as late as midnight.

Going to a "fancy dress ball" meant wearing a costume. Many children dressed as shepherds, dairymaids, and jesters in the 1850s.

Today, parades mark the end of Carnival in New Orleans. When Marie-Grace's story takes place, balls were the highlight of the Mardi Gras season. There were different balls for children and for adults. The children's balls took place early in the evening in the same ballrooms that later hosted balls for the adults. Some grown-ups were so eager to dance that they joined the children. When it got too crowded, the adults had to be told to wait their turn!

There were also separate balls for white people and for people of color, though they were often held in the same buildings. For all ages and colors, the magical part of Mardi Gras was dressing up and dancing. As

Marie-Grace and Cécile discovered, putting on costumes and masks gave people a chance for mischievous adventures and memorable celebrations.

Many of the things that made New Orleans different from the rest of America in the 1850s are still part of the city's charm and character today. The mix of cultures that shaped its history can be seen in the architecture, music, food, and people that make New Orleans the unique and vibrant city it is.

Glossary of French Words

arbre *(ar-bruh)*—tree

au revoir *(oh ruh-vwar)*—good-bye

baguette *(bah-get)*—a long, thin loaf of French bread

banquette *(bahn-ket)*—sidewalk

bien sûr *(byehn sewr)*—of course

bon *(bohn)*—good

bonjour *(bohn-zhoor)*—hello

bonne nuit *(bun nwee)*—good night

certainement *(sehr-ten-mahn)*—certainly

chérie *(shay-ree)*—dear, darling

Comment vas-tu? *(koh-mahn vah-tew)*—How are you?

filé *(fee-lay)*—a flavorful powder that is sprinkled into soups and stews to thicken them. It is made from the dried and ground leaves of the sassafras tree.

gens de couleur libres *(zhahn duh koo-luhr lee-bruh)*—free people of color

mademoiselle *(mahd-mwah-zel)*—Miss, young lady

magnifique *(mah-nyee-feek)*—beautiful, magnificent

maman *(mah-mahn)*—mother, mama

Mardi Gras (*mar-dee grah*)—a day of feasting and parties just before the somber religious period called Lent begins. "Mardi Gras season" refers to the several weeks of festivities leading up to Mardi Gras. The words *Mardi Gras* mean "fat Tuesday."

merci (*mehr-see*)—thank you

mon frère (*mohn frehr*)—my brother

monsieur (*muh-syuh*)—Mister, sir

non (*nohn*)—no

oui (*wee*)—yes

pommes de terre (*pum duh tehr*)—potatoes

praline (*prah-leen*)—a rich, sweet treat made of pecans, brown sugar, and butter

très bien (*treh byehn*)—very good, very well

Une banquette, s'il vous plaît. (*ewn bahn-ket seel voo pleh*)—A sidewalk, please. (A silly request that Marie-Grace makes by mistake)

How to Pronounce French Names

Belle Chênière *(bel sheh-nyehr)*

Cécile Rey *(say-seel ray)*

Eléanore *(ay-lay-uh-nor)*

Grand Théâtre *(grahn tay-ah-truh)*

Louis *(loo-ee)*

Luc Rousseau *(lewk roo-soh)*

Monsieur Bernard *(muh-syuh behr-nar)*

Océane Michel *(oh-say-ahn mee-shel)*

Octavia *(ohk-tah-vyah)*

Réne *(ruh-nay)*

Ti-Marie *(tee-mah-ree)*—Marie-Grace's nickname. "Ti" is
    short for *petite*, or "little," so the nickname means
    "Little Marie."

GET THE WHOLE STORY

Two very different girls share a unique friendship and a remarkable story. Cécile's and Marie-Grace's books take turns describing the year that changes both their lives. Read all six!

Available at bookstores and at *americangirl.com*

BOOK 1: MEET MARIE-GRACE
When Marie-Grace arrives in New Orleans, she's not sure she fits in—until an unexpected invitation opens the door to friendship.

BOOK 2: MEET CÉCILE
Cécile plans a secret adventure at a glittering costume ball. But her daring plan won't work unless Marie-Grace is brave enough to take part, too!

BOOK 3: MARIE-GRACE AND THE ORPHANS
Marie-Grace discovers an abandoned baby. With Cécile's help, she finds a safe place for him. But when a fever threatens the city, she wonders if *anyone* will be safe.

BOOK 4: TROUBLES FOR CÉCILE
Yellow fever spreads through the city—and into Cécile's own home. Marie-Grace offers help, but it's up to Cécile to be strong when her family needs her most.

BOOK 5: MARIE-GRACE MAKES A DIFFERENCE
As the fever rages on, Marie-Grace and Cécile volunteer at a crowded orphanage. Then Marie-Grace discovers that it's not just the orphans who need help.

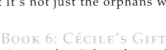

BOOK 6: CÉCILE'S GIFT
The epidemic is over, but it has changed Cécile—and New Orleans—forever. With Marie-Grace's encouragement, Cécile steps onstage to help her beloved city recover.

A SNEAK PEEK AT

THE NEXT BOOK IN THE SERIES

MEET

Cécile

In the quiet parlor, Cécile's pen scratched across paper as she worked on a letter to her brother, Armand. Nearby, Maman and Tante Octavia, Cécile's aunt, did needlework, and Cochon, the parrot, dozed on his perch.

Cécile dotted her last *i* and held her paper up to catch the fading afternoon light. It would have been easier to see if she'd started earlier in the day, the way Maman had wanted. But, she realized with a smile, Armand wouldn't mind messy handwriting.

Dear Armand,

Do you miss me as much as I miss you? I hope you had a wonderful Christmas in Paris. Is it snowing there? I wish I could see snow! All we have in New Orleans is rain, rain, rain. At least the Mardi Gras parties start soon. I don't know what costume to wear to the Children's Ball. I wish you were here to help me decide. You always have the best ideas!

Here is some news—I was the star of a play today! Well, it was only one scene, and

there was no stage or costumes, but no matter.
I acted out a scene from a play for all my
friends at La Maison. I managed to play three
characters and make them all quite different.
Everyone laughed at the funny parts and
applauded when I was done. They said I was
very good. I'll perform the scene for you when
you come home—I hope you'll like it, too.

Well, I must go now. Everything else is
very boring. Besides, Maman complains when
I use too much of her ink—and then she also
complains when I don't write! So what am I to
do? Anyway, everyone sends love. I'm counting
the days until you come home—

Your loving sister,

Cécé

Cécile slipped her letter into a stiff envelope.
Then she pressed a little wax flower onto the flap
to seal it tight. Would Armand open her letter the
minute it arrived, as she did his?

"Very good, Cécile," Maman said from across
the parlor. "Now, *ma petite*, about Mardi Gras. Why
not be a princess for the ball?" Maman's knitting

needles clicked as she spoke.

"Oh, Maman, not a princess again!" Cécile turned and her little cousin, René, squealed and ran to her, tipping the basket of yarn that his mother was using for her needlework. Cécile quickly got down onto her knees to collect the tumbling balls of yarn.

Tante Octavia stopped her needlepoint to watch Cécile scoop up a handful of pink wool. "You would look lovely in that shade of pink," she said to her niece.

Cécile looked at the yarn against the golden brown of her hand. The pink *would* look perfect, but...

"Monette Bruiller's mother has ordered a pink princess costume for her," Cécile said. "I want to be *une originale* for Mardi Gras—like no one else!"

Papa came in laughing from the hallway. "Cécile, you *are* une originale," he said. "You're my one and only daughter!" He shrugged off his heavy coat as their new maid, Ellen, a young Irish girl, stood waiting to hang it up. Then he crossed the cozy room to kiss Maman.

"Papa!" Cécile jumped up to give him a hug. "You're home early today," she said happily, following Papa across the thick carpet.

Papa sank into his chair. Cécile leaned against

his arm and sneezed as a tiny puff of marble dust floated into her nose. Papa designed and carved beautiful things out of marble: statues that seemed almost alive, fancy urns and stately grave markers,

marble urn

even fireplace mantels for homes and businesses. He spent long hours at his stone yard, and he was very successful.

"We finished a job ahead of schedule, so I came home to enjoy my Cécé's chatter," he said fondly. "And just think, when Armand is back from Paris and we're working together, we'll finish early more often!"

Cécile was quiet for a moment. She missed Armand the most when everyone was together like this. "Armand will be a great stonemason, just like you, Papa," she said.

"Just like you!" René shouted, running to wrap his fat little arms around Papa's legs. Papa patted René's black curls and looked across the room.

"How are you today, Octavia?" he asked gently.

Cécile looked up to see that her aunt had lowered her head over her work, unable to find her voice to

Cécile was quiet for a moment. She missed Armand the most when everyone was together like this.

answer Papa back. Cécile knew that Tante, who
had been widowed only six months ago, missed
her husband terribly. Most days she was laughing,
but sometimes she became very sad. This was one
of those times.

At that moment, Cochon
flapped his bright wings and
squawked. Cécile suddenly thought
of a way to cheer up her aunt. She
tapped her father's arm excitedly.

"Oh, Papa, I know what my
Mardi Gras costume will be," Cécile joked, clapping
her hands. "I will be a bird!" she announced. "A
great, noisy bird."

"A bird! A bird!" the big parrot squawked loudly.
Laughing, Cécile ducked as he swooped across the
room to land on her shoulder.

"A bird!" Maman took off her eyeglasses as
she looked up from her knitting. "Cécile, you didn't
say . . . a bird?"

"I think she did, Aurélia!" Papa chuckled.

"Cécile, wouldn't you look charming wearing
a parrot's beak to the ball!" said Tante Tay. She was
smiling now.

"I'm a bird, too," René shouted. He pranced around Cécile with his arms spread like wings. Cécile flapped her hands and chased after him, squawking like Cochon.

"You really must stop playing that way, Cécile. Behave like a lady," Maman scolded gently, shaking her head.

Cécile captured her little cousin, who giggled and shrieked as she tickled him. Just then her grandfather peered into the noisy parlor.

"*Quelle horreur!* What a fright!" Grand-pére boomed, pretending to be shocked. Ellen peeked into the parlor over his shoulder.

Cochon flew over to them and flapped rudely in Ellen's face. "Off with you, wild thing!" Ellen cried, batting him away with her apron. Then she bobbed in a curtsy to Maman. "Sorry, ma'am. I don't have much experience with birdhouses," she said solemnly, but the corners of her eyes crinkled with amusement.

"Grand-père," Cécile giggled, "welcome to our birdhouse!"

Maman sniffed, as a proper lady might in such a wild house. Then she winked at Cécile.

"Ellen," Maman said, smiling, "the birds would now like to have hot chocolate!"

Cécile burst out laughing at Maman's silliness. Oh, how she wished she could share this happy moment with Armand.

Meet Marie-Grace

DATE DUE
